Mr. Greg's Ospreys

by:

Laura Callahan
Jill Waldman
Patrice Boone

Illustrated by: Christine Williams

AuthorHouse™
1663 Liberty Drive
Bloomington, IN 47403
www.authorhouse.com
Phone: 833-262-8899

Because of the dynamic nature of the Internet, any web addresses or links contained in this book may have changed
since publication and may no longer be valid. The views expressed in this work are solely those of the author and do not
necessarily reflect the views of the publisher, and the publisher hereby disclaims any responsibility for them.

Any people depicted in stock imagery provided by Getty Images are models,
and such images are being used for illustrative purposes only.
Certain stock imagery © Getty Images.

This book is printed on acid-free paper.

ISBN: 978-1-6655-2092-8 (sc)
ISBN: 978-1-6655-2091-1 (hc)
ISBN: 978-1-6655-2093-5 (e)

Library of Congress Control Number: 2021906273

Print information available on the last page.

Published by AuthorHouse 03/29/2021

authorHOUSE®

The authors would like to thank Christine Williams for her extraordinary artistic talent displayed through the beautiful illustrations contained in this book. She brought our story and the beauty of Jug Bay on the Patuxent River to life!

The authors would also like to thank Kelly Callahan for her artistic touches and technical expertise in organizing and formatting the many pages of text and illustrations.

Laura Callahan would like to personally thank her amazing co-authors, Jill Waldman and Patrice Boone for their creativity, patience and love! By agreeing to take this journey with me, Mr. Greg's Ospreys became a reality and fulfilled a long-awaited dream!

This is Mr. Greg. He has a very special job. Mr. Greg manages an osprey sanctuary on Jug Bay on the Patuxent River in Maryland! Dressed in his khaki shirt and pants, floppy brimmed hat and sunglasses, he is easy to spot on his boat.

With natural habitats being lost to development and a changing climate, Mr. Greg works hard all year long to make sure his ospreys have everything they need to nest and raise their chicks on Jug Bay.

On a humid, mid-July morning, Mr. Greg watches as the first of his ospreys take flight. With their hawk-like bodies, these large fish-eating birds of prey begin their long migration south. They travel very far from Jug Bay to Florida, Cuba, and even the northern regions of South America up to 4000 miles away!

Mr. Greg tracks the ospreys' migration by communicating with other conservationists. They send him information about his birds' condition throughout their long journey and while they winter in warmer climates. The youngest ospreys will spend their first two years in these warm regions before returning to Jug Bay as adults.

As winter arrives, Mr. Greg begins preparing for his ospreys' return in spring. Winter brings ice, snow and wind that can damage the nesting towers. In late winter, he takes his boat into the frigid water to inspect each tower for any damage.

Mr. Greg notices a nesting tower that is leaning a bit and stops to examine it more closely. Kneeling down in his boat next to the tower, he sees the support beam is cracked. Using a brace, he attaches it to the broken beam so the tower is once again sturdy and safe for his ospreys to nest. He will make needed repairs to all the towers by early March.

As winter comes to an end and the last of the frost disappears, Mr. Greg waits with excitement for his ospreys to return from their winter homes! Sadly, not all his ospreys will make it back. Storms, wind turbines, predators, and other obstacles may cause an early end to their journey. He will watch over Jug Bay each day for his ospreys' spring arrival. As his birds return, Mr. Greg can monitor their activities from the webcam in his office.

The day has finally come. After months of preparation and waiting, Mr. Greg spots his first osprey on the horizon! It is a male osprey that has nested here before and will return to the same nest as last year.

The male osprey will wait in his nest for the return of his mate. A few days later, the female osprey joins him.

Each day, Mr. G_____ ____s return to _____ until most of the nests are ____ ____s, ___stalks, grasses and odd scr__s th_ ____ ____ ____uild their nests. One osprey p___s __ ____ pr__dly in the nest!

In April and May, the female ospreys lay their cream and brown speckled eggs. They blend in perfectly with their nest so they are not seen by predators. Occasionally, Mr. Greg takes a boat ride on the peaceful waters of Jug Bay to check the nesting osprey pairs and their eggs. He takes a logbook along to record all of his observations.

By the second week of May, Mr. Greg takes his boat to check the nests. It happened! The osprey eggs have hatched! The chicks are tiny and covered in brown and tan down feathers. Just like their eggs, the coloring will camouflage them within the nest so they are not easily seen. The down feathers do not protect them from the heat of the sun, so their mother will use her broad wings to shade them and keep them cool.

For up to six weeks, the mother osprey sits on the nest all day and night. The father will sit on the nest for a short time each day to give the mother a rest. The parents will never leave the chicks alone. The chicks know to crouch low and stay still so they will not be seen by predators.

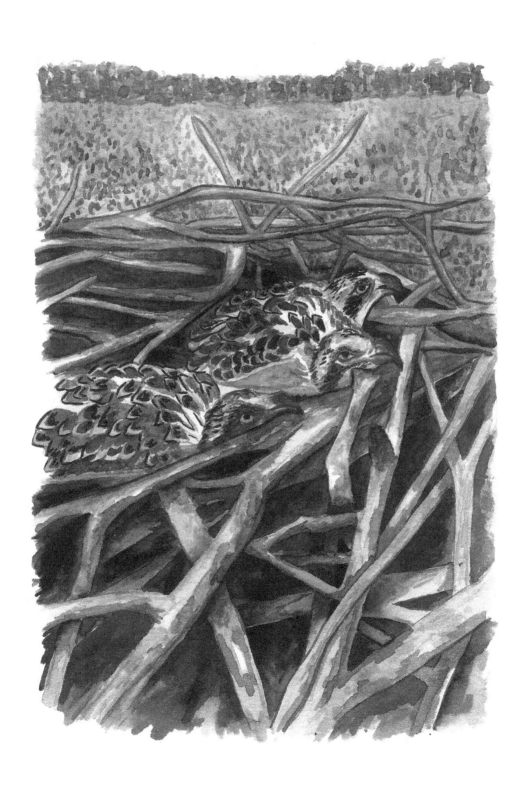

Late one night, a great horned owl, one of the ospreys' fiercest predators, circles a nest with a mother and her chicks. The owl sets its sight on one of the chicks for its evening meal.

Fortunately, the osprey chicks' mother is there to defend them. She swoops at the great horned owl with her talons ready to attack and chases the owl far away from the nest! Mr. Greg knows some chicks may not be spared from the owl's nightly hunts. He is sad when this happens but understands this is part of nature. The owl also has to feed its young.

Today, as Mr. Greg watches from his boat, he sees a male osprey soar into the sky and then swiftly dive toward the water! Plunging feet first and using his sharp talons, he grabs a fish and carries it back to the nest to eat and share with his mate. The mother will tear tiny pieces of the fish to feed to her chicks.

By late June and early July, the osprey chicks have grown much bigger! Mr. Greg sees the young chicks flapping their wings. They are not ready to fly, but the flapping helps their wing muscles grow stronger in preparation for their first flight.

When they are one month old, Mr. Greg starts placing identification bands on each osprey chick. This takes several weeks as there are over 100 chicks! As he steers his boat toward a nest, the mother osprey will fly a short distance to keep watch as the banding takes place.

Mr. Greg carefully takes one of the osprey chicks from its nest to the boat.
With help from volunteers or wild-life assistants, Mr. Greg weighs each
chick and places a small numbered aluminum band on its leg. This does
not hurt the chick. The band will identify the osprey and help track it
when it migrates south at the end of the summer and for the rest of its life.

At six weeks of age, the chicks are fully feathered. As they continue to grow, they are able to eat with much less help from their parents. The osprey chicks watch the adult ospreys fish throughout the day. Mr. Greg knows they will soon learn to fish on their own.

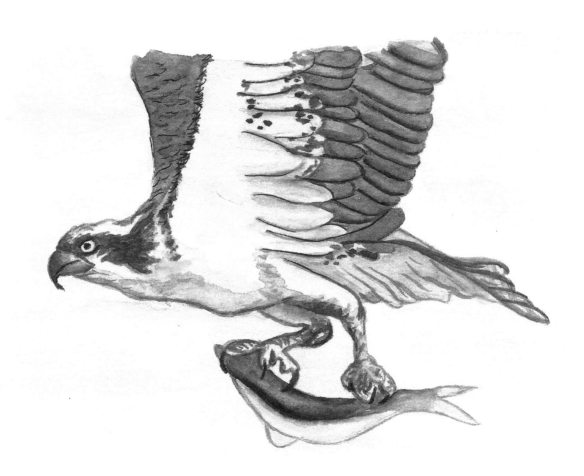

It is now the middle of July and the chicks are eight weeks old. Mr. Greg watches from his boat as a young osprey flaps its wings and takes flight for the first time! He sees other young ospreys taking their first flights too. The chicks have grown up with the care of their parents and under Mr. Greg's watchful eye. They are ready to start life on their own.

In late August, Mr. Greg waves goodbye to his ospreys as they once again leave for their winter migration. He will miss his osprey friends. He thinks about the challenges he and his ospreys have overcome this year and those his birds will face again during their long journey south. Mr. Greg is both happy and proud of the work he has done to make sure these beautiful ospreys always have a home to return to and raise their families on Jug Bay!

To readers of Mr. Greg's Ospreys:

You are never too young to be a conservationist like Mr. Greg! By planting trees and flowers, recycling and keeping the environment clean, you can help preserve habitats for wildlife too!

Dedication

The authors dedicate "Mr. Greg's Ospreys" to Greg Kearns, whose conservation efforts to support the osprey population served as the inspiration for this book.

Greg is a Park Naturalist who manages osprey nesting towers that are part of the Jug Bay Natural Area on the Patuxent River near Upper Marlboro under the Maryland-National Capital Park and Planning Commission. Greg, a master bird bander, established the osprey nesting site program in 1984 under the mentorship of fellow naturalist and bird bander Steve Cardano and park director Rich Dolesh as there was a critical need for nesting platforms to reestablish the osprey population on the Patuxent River. Natural predators, suburban sprawl, pollution, effects of past use of DDT, lack of nesting sites and climate change have negatively impacted the ability of the ospreys to reproduce. Ospreys are birds of prey near the top of the food web and are important environmental indicators of the health of lakes, rivers and estuaries around the world. Through Greg's tireless efforts, osprey populations have grown and continue to flourish on the Patuxent River.

Greg received his Bachelor of Science in Biology in 1983 from Saint Mary's College of Maryland and has worked for almost 40 years at the Patuxent River Park, Jug Bay Natural Area.

This book highlights and honors Greg for his ongoing work to assure ospreys continue to thrive and remain an integral part of the Patuxent ecosystem.

CPSIA information can be obtained
at www.ICGtesting.com
Printed in the USA
LVHW070022050521
686549LV00018B/1607